Parents and Caregive[rs]

Stone Arch Readers are designed to pr[ovide] experiences, as well as opportunities to [develo]p vocabulary, literacy skills, and comprehension. Here are a few ways to support your beginning reader:

- Talk with your child about the ideas addressed in the story.

- Discuss each illustration, mentioning the characters, where they are, and what they are doing.

- Read with expression, pointing to each word. You may want to read the whole story through and then revisit parts of the story to ensure that the meanings of words or phrases are understood.

- Talk about why the character did what he or she did and what your child would do in that situation.

- Help your child connect with characters and events in the story.

Remember, reading with your child should be fun, not forced. Each moment spent reading with your child is a priceless investment in his or her literacy life.

Gail Saunders-Smith, Ph.D.

Stone Arch Readers

are published by Stone Arch Books
a Capstone Imprint
1710 Roe Crest Drive
North Mankato, Minnesota 56003
www.capstonepub.com

Library of Congress Cataloging-in-Publication Data
Crow, Melinda Melton.
Rocky and Daisy go camping / by Melinda Melton Crow; illustrated by Mike Brownlow.
p. cm. — (Stone Arch readers: My two dogs)
Summary: Rocky and Daisy go on a camping trip with their human family.
ISBN 978-1-4342-4162-7 (library binding)
ISBN 978-1-4342-6117-5 (paperback)
1. Dogs—Juvenile fiction. 2. Camping—Juvenile fiction. [1. Dogs—Fiction. 2. Camping—Fiction.]
I. Brownlow, Michael, ill. II. Title.
PZ7.C88536Rph 2013
813.6—dc23am   2012027140

Reading Consultants:
Gail Saunders-Smith, Ph.D.
Melinda Melton Crow, M.Ed.
Laurie K. Holland, Media Specialist

Designer: Russell Griesmer

Printed in the United States of America in Stevens Point, Wisconsin.
092012
006937WZS13

Rocky and Daisy
Go Camping

by Melinda Melton Crow
illustrated by Mike Brownlow

STONE ARCH BOOKS
a capstone imprint

MY TWO DOGS

I'm Owen, and these are Rocky and Daisy, my two dogs.

ROCKY LIKES:

- Chasing squirrels
- Playing with other dogs
- Chewing things
- Running with me when I ride my bike

DAISY LIKES:

- Playing ball
- Listening to stories
- Resting on the furniture
- Eating yummy treats

Owen did everything with his dogs. When Owen went on bike rides, Rocky ran along.

When Owen read a story,
Daisy listened.

Owen's family was going
camping soon.

"This year, we'll take Rocky
and Daisy, too," said Mom.

"Yay!" yelled Owen.

Camping was always fun.
But it would be even better with
Rocky and Daisy.

Getting ready for the trip was a lot of work. Dad found the tent and the sleeping bags.

Mom packed the clothes and the food.

Owen helped carry everything
out to the camper.

Everyone climbed in the van.
Daisy was nervous. She did not
like cars.

"Let's sing a song," said
Mom. "That will make Daisy
feel better."

They sang the whole way.
Even Daisy sang along.

At the campground, Rocky
and Daisy sniffed and sniffed.
The mountain air smelled like
pine trees and campfires.

"I like camping," said Rocky.

"Me too," said Daisy.

Owen helped Dad put up the tent. "You can sleep here with Rocky and Daisy," said Dad. "Mom and I will sleep in the camper."

"Oh, boy!" said Owen.
"Sleeping in the tent with my
dogs will be fun."

After everything was set up, it
was time for some fun!

"Let's go swimming!" said
Owen.

They ran down to the beach.
Owen and Rocky jumped in.
But Daisy was nervous.

"Come on, Daisy," said Rocky.
He splashed her until she was
swimming, too.

After swimming, they played
ball. Owen threw the ball as
far as he could. Daisy and
Rocky chased after it. They were
racing!

Daisy reached the ball first,
but just barely!

"We need some wood for a fire," said Mom.

"Let's go hiking and gather sticks," said Dad.

Owen and his dogs explored the hiking trail. They saw rabbits. They heard a woodpecker. They smelled wildflowers.

Soon, everyone was hungry.
They cooked hot dogs over the
fire.

"Those hot dogs smell so
good," said Rocky.

He snuck closer to Mom's hot dog.

"No, Rocky," said Mom. "You have your own food."

"Aw, man," said Rocky.

When it got dark, Rocky and
Daisy yawned. They went and
stood by the tent.

"Time for bed," said Dad.

Owen crawled into the tent with the dogs. They snuggled up and went to sleep.

Suddenly, thunder boomed!
Rocky and Daisy woke up.

"I'm scared," Daisy howled.

Owen woke up, too. "Let's go sleep with Mom and Dad," he said.

They all ran to the camper.

Owen and the dogs snuggled in next to Mom and Dad.

"It is better to all be together anyway," said Owen.

Mom and Dad were not sure they agreed.

THE END

STORY WORDS

sniffed	woodpecker	snuggled
barely	wildflowers	thunder
explored	snuck	howled

Total Word Count: 432

READ MORE
ROCKY AND DAISY ADVENTURES!